For the whole "zoo": R.J., Ryan, Raina, Shae, Scarlet, Owen,
and (of course) Clarke (and Lucky and Phoenix)! —C. R.

For my two adventurous pups, Winter and Autumn —M. P.

First published in the United States of America in November 2015 by Bloomsbury Children's Books
www.bloomsbury.com

Bloomsbury is a registered trademark of Bloomsbury Publishing Plc

For information about permission to reproduce selections from this book, write to Permissions, Bloomsbury Children's Books, 1385 Broadway, New York, New York 10018
Bloomsbury books may be purchased for business or promotional use. For information on bulk purchases please contact Macmillan Corporate and Premium Sales Department at specialmarkets@macmillan.com

Library of Congress Cataloging-in-Publication Data
Ryan, Candace.
Zoo zoom! / by Candace Ryan ; illustrated by Macky Pamintuan.
pages   cm
Summary: The animals at the zoo have a great idea—to take a rocket into outer space! But this flight of fancy goes awry when the rhino falls asleep on the job. Will they be able to return safely to Earth? Zoo zoom, zoo moon!
ISBN 978-1-61963-357-5 (hardcover) • ISBN 978-1-61963-815-0 (e-book) • ISBN 978-1-61963-816-7 (e-PDF)
[1. Space flight—Fiction. 2. Zoo animals—Fiction.] I. Pamintuan, Macky, illustrator. II. Title.
PZ8.3.R945Zo 2015   [E]—dc23   2014038763

Art created digitally • Typeset in Gill Sans Mt Std • Book design by Yelena Safronova
Printed in China by Leo Paper Products, Heshan, Guangdong
1 3 5 7 9 10 8 6 4 2

ZOO ZOOM!

Candace Ryan • illustrated by **Macky Pamintuan**

BLOOMSBURY
NEW YORK   LONDON   NEW DELHI   SYDNEY

Monkey turns the key.
Condor opens door.

Which bar to go far?

zoo **ZOOM!**
zoo **ZOOM!**

Puffin flies in.
Cockatoo, too.

Buffalo shifts low.
Pronghorn hits the horn.

Crocodile sets the dial.

Yak yack-yack . . .

Which knob for the job?

Flamingo calls, "Go!"

Kiwi cries, "Whee!"

Which seat can't be beat?

Hippo shouts, "Oh!
Rhino, no!"

Which switch? Don't twitch!

ZOO DOOM!
ZOO DOOM!

Toucan can do.

Cockatoo takes two.

Which track to get back?

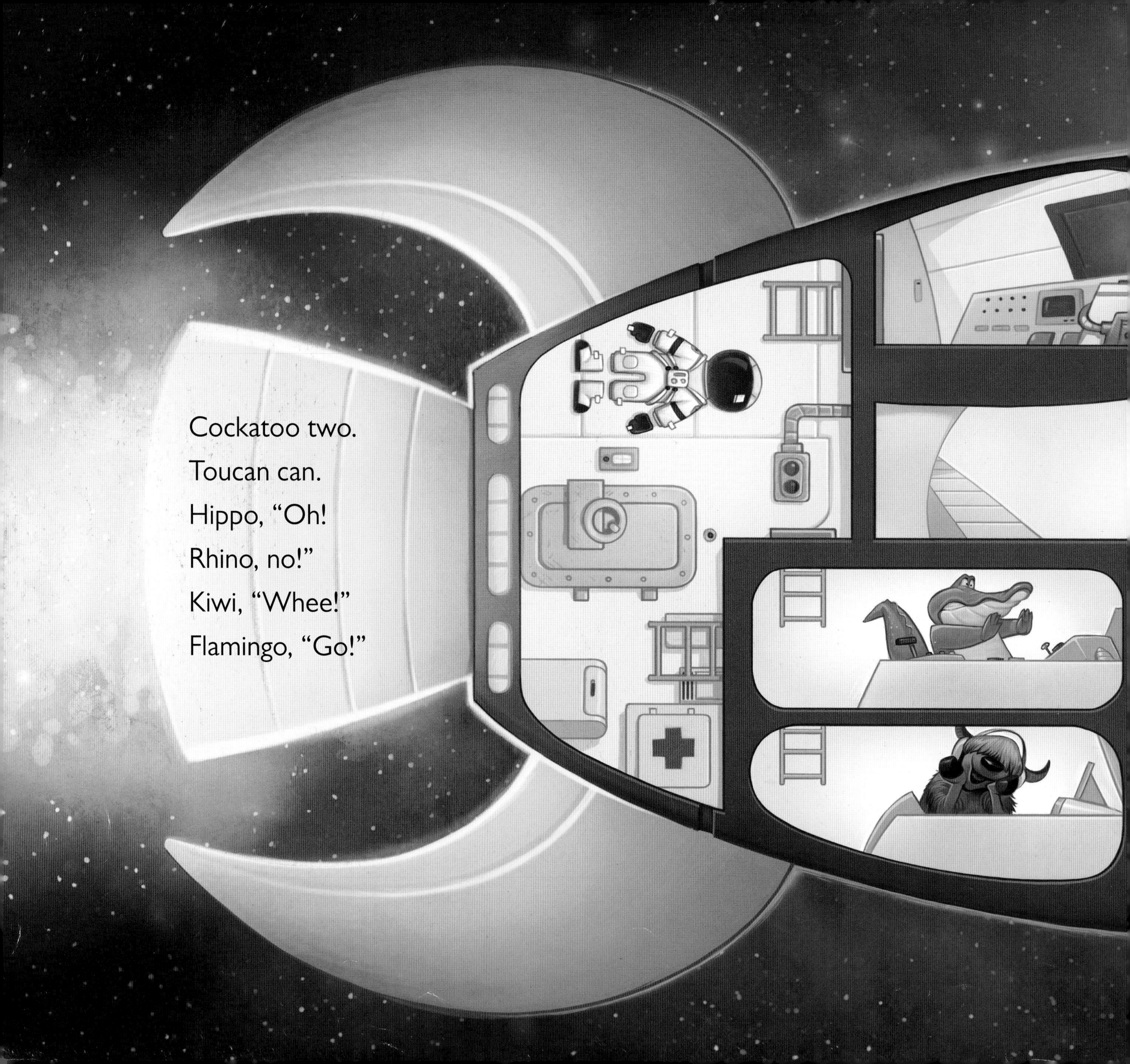

Cockatoo two.

Toucan can.

Hippo, "Oh!

Rhino, no!"

Kiwi, "Whee!"

Flamingo, "Go!"

ZOO SOON! ZOO SOON!

Yak yack-yack . . .

Crocodile dial.

Pronghorn horn.

Buffalo low.

Cockatoo, too.

Puffin in.

Condor door.

Monkey key.

Which beds for sleepy heads?

ZOO SNOOZE.
ZOO SNOOZE.

So until the next zoo zoom,

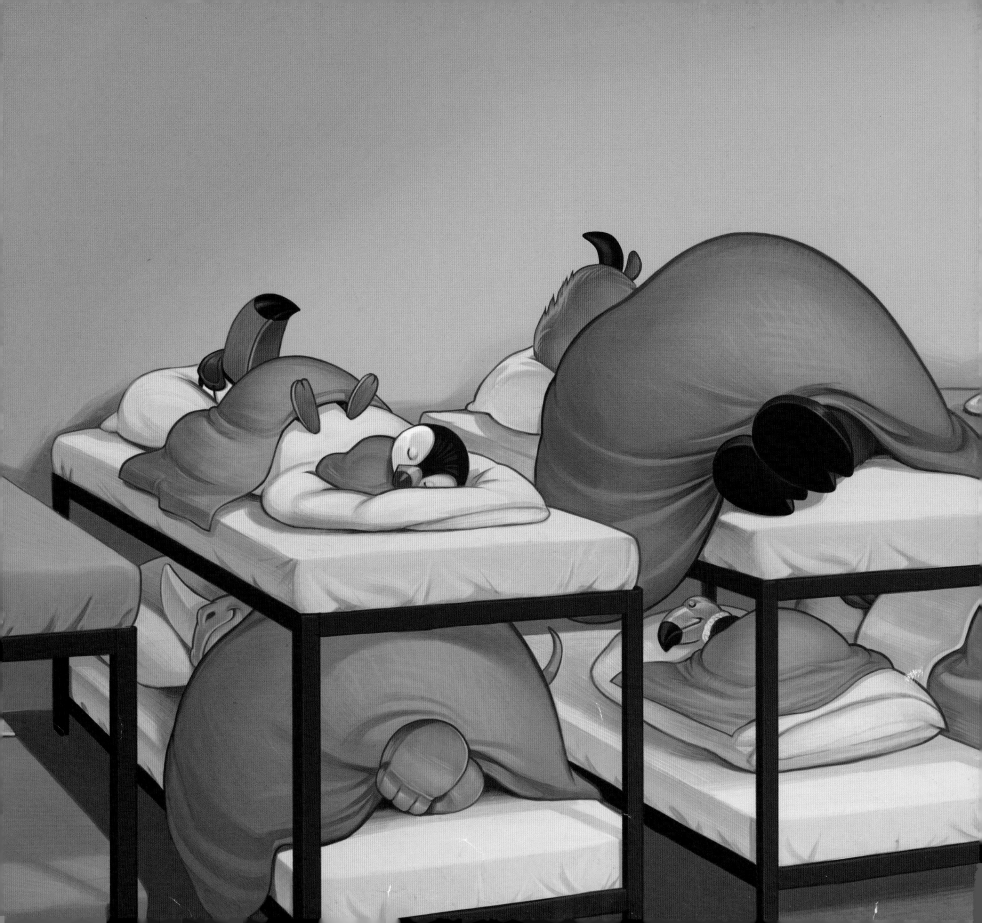

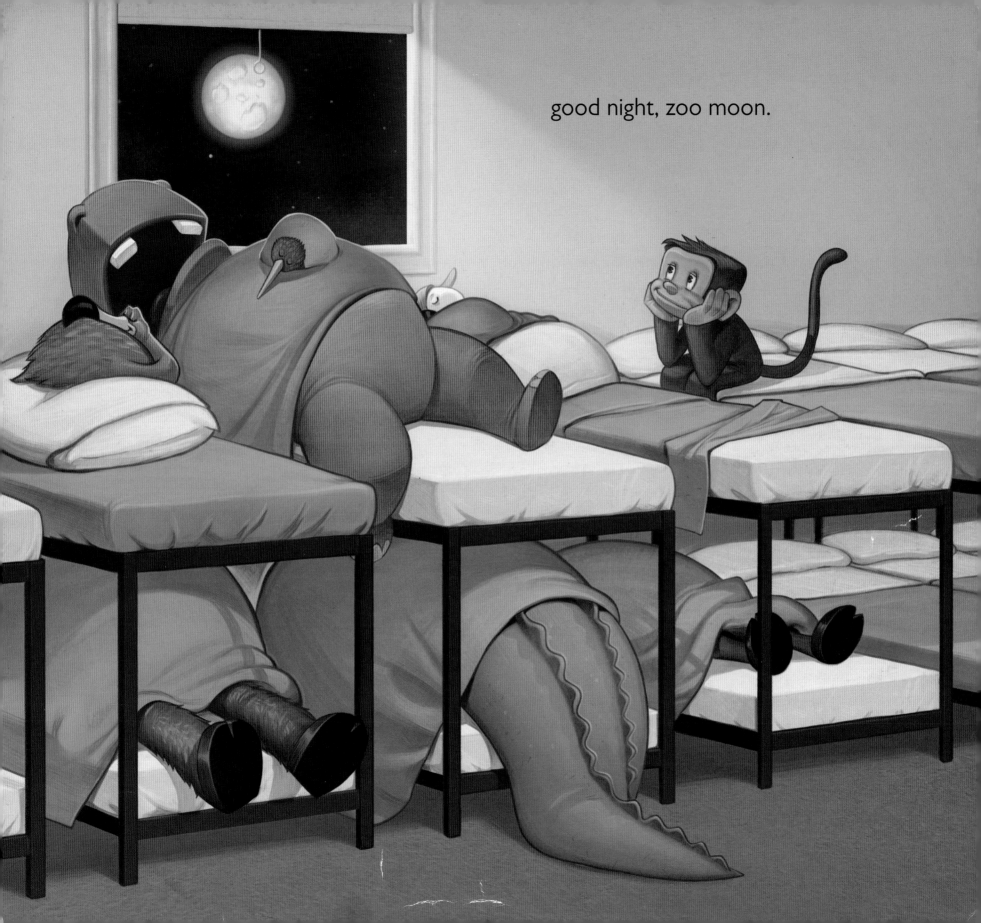

good night, zoo moon.